D1094895

Why Are You So Quiet?

Story by
Jaclyn Desforges

Art by
Risa Hugo

annick press
toronto • berkeley

Myra Louise was a quiet girl who loved quiet places.

She loved building forts in her room on rainy days.

She loved listening to the crickets croon from her backyard tree at sunset.

She loved the gentle hum of the dryers at the laundromat.

In fact, Myra Louise loved quietness
so much that even the loudest words
she spoke came out slow and soft.

And so everywhere Myra Louise went, people asked the same question.

Why are you so quiet?

On the school bus, her classmate Jeremy
sidled up to her and screeched it.

When she didn't raise her hand in class, Mr. Bellman
scrunched up his eyebrows and demanded it.

And when she hid in her room
to read while company was over,
her mom opened the door and sighed it.

And Myra Louise didn't know
quite how to answer.

And so Myra Louise started to
feel smaller and smaller.

So she thought very hard, because Myra Louise was a very good thinker.

She thought if she could just find the answer to their question, everyone would finally understand.

At the laundromat, Myra Louise sat next to the quietest dryer.
She listened and thought for a long, long time.

Then she whispered,
"Dryer, why are you so quiet?"

The dryer didn't answer—she didn't think so, anyway. The gentle sounds of tossing and tumbling were so muffled that Myra Louise wasn't quite sure.

Then, she got an idea.

She started collecting things she noticed,
because Myra Louise was a very good noticer.

She collected copper wire and bits of string
and lost buttons and tinfoil.

She collected seashells and tiny
stones and egg cartons and wool.

And she started reading, because Myra Louise was a very good reader.

She read books about inventing and engineering and creating.

She read books about machines and about tinkering and building.

LISTENING MACHINE

And she went to the garage, the quietest place in the whole house. The hours fell away as she glued and fastened and hammered.

Before she knew it, she had made . . .

. . . a listening machine.

Myra Louise beamed at her creation.

A single earpiece poked out from
a tangle of overlooked objects,
all connected to a big red switch.

Raindrops drummed softly against the roof.
Myra Louise pulled on her raincoat and went outside.

Then she switched on her listening machine,
placed the earpiece against her ear, and whispered,
"Raindrops, why are you so quiet?"

The rain didn't answer.

But its pitter-patter was so mesmerizing through the listening machine that she stood there peacefully for almost an hour.

After the rain had passed, Myra Louise climbed up in her backyard elm tree and switched on her listening machine.

Through the machine, the crickets' evening song was the most beautiful music her ears had ever heard.

She didn't need an
answer anymore.

She just wished someone
else could listen, too.

Before bed, Myra Louise tiptoed back to the garage to make one slight adjustment.

As Mom tucked her in,
Myra Louise switched on her
listening machine again.

This time, there were two earpieces.

Even though Mom was yawning,
the story she read sounded so magical to
both of them that they decided to stay
up late and read two extra chapters.

The next day, Myra Louise brought her new-and-improved listening machine to school.

At recess, she crouched down in the grass and listened to the sound of a ladybug fluttering her wings.

Just then, her classmate Jeremy
came up to her and hollered,
"Why are you so quiet?"

"Shh," Myra Louise said.
"I'm listening."

Then Jeremy crouched down to listen, too.

For my daughter, Quinn, for my younger self, and for quiet kids everywhere.
—J.D.

For Q, J, and you.
—R.H.

We acknowledge the support of the Canada Council for the Arts and the Ontario Arts Council, and the participation of the Government of Canada/la participation du gouvernement du Canada for our publishing activities.

ONTARIO ARTS COUNCIL
CONSEIL DES ARTS DE L'ONTARIO
an Ontario government agency
un organisme du gouvernement de l'Ontario

Library and Archives Canada Cataloguing in Publication

Title: Why are you so quiet? / story by Jaclyn Desforges ; art by Risa Hugo.
Names: Desforges, Jaclyn, 1988- author. | Hugo, Risa, 1990- illustrator.
Identifiers: Canadiana (print) 20200193899 | Canadiana (ebook) 20200193945 | ISBN 9781773214344 (hardcover) | ISBN 9781773214375 (PDF) | ISBN 9781773214351 (HTML) | ISBN 9781773214368 (Kindle)
Classification: LCC PS8607.E75815 W59 2020 | DDC jC813/.6—dc23

Published in the U.S.A. by Annick Press (U.S.) Ltd.
Distributed in Canada by University of Toronto Press.
Distributed in the U.S.A. by Publishers Group West.

Printed in China

annickpress.com
jaclyndesforges.me
risahugo.com

Also available as an e-book. Please visit annickpress.com/ebooks for more details.

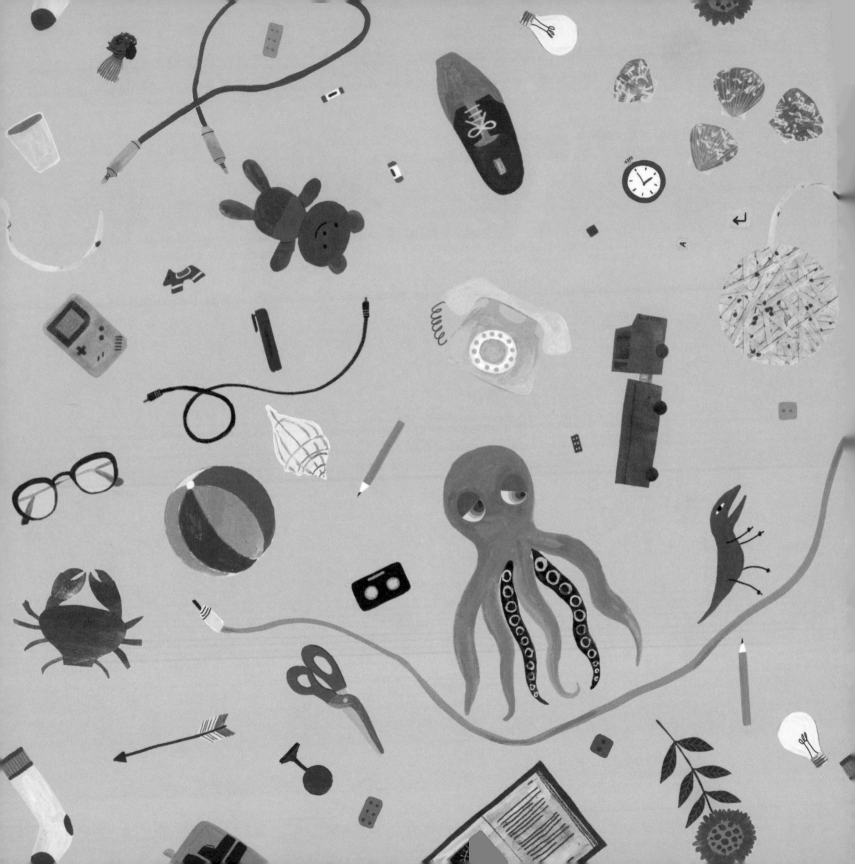